Gargoylz

on the Loose!

Gargoylz: grotesque stone creatures found on old buildings, spouting rainwater from the guttering. Sometimes seen causing mischief and mayhem before scampering away over rooftops.

www.kidsatrandomhouse.co.uk

Read all the
Gargoylz adventures!

Gargoylz on the Loose!

Gargoylz Get Up to Mischief

Gargoylz at a Midnight Feast

Gargoylz Take a Trip

Gargoylz

on the Loose!

Burchett & Vogler

illustrated by Leighton Noyes

RED FOX

GARGOYLZ ON THE LOOSE!
A RED FOX BOOK 978 1 862 30835 0

First published in Great Britain by Red Fox,
an imprint of Random House Children's Books
A Random House Group Company

This edition published 2009

1 3 5 7 9 10 8 6 4 2

Series created and developed by Amber Caravéo
Copyright © Random House Children's Books, 2009

The Random House Group Limited supports the Forest Stewardship
Council (FSC), the leading international forest certification organization.
All our titles that are printed on Greenpeace-approved FSC-certified paper
carry the FSC logo. Our paper procurement policy can be found at
www.rbooks.co.uk/environment

Set in Bembo Schoolbook

Red Fox Books are published by Random House Children's Books,
61–63 Uxbridge Road, London W5 5SA

www.**kids**at**randomhouse**.co.uk
www.**rbooks**.co.uk

Addresses for companies within The Random House Group Limited can be
found at: www.randomhouse.co.uk/offices.htm

THE RANDOM HOUSE GROUP Limited Reg. No. 954009

A CIP catalogue record for this book is available from the British Library.

Printed and bound in Great Britain by CPI Bookmarque, Croydon, CR0 4TD

For Amber Caravéo, for being so lovely to work with, and without whom the Gargoylz would not have come to life
– **Burchett & Vogler**

For Elodie who designed Toby,
with all my love forever, Daddy x
– **Leighton Noyes**

Hello, I'm the Web Gargoyle.
Look out for me – I'll be hiding in one of the pictures in the book.
When you spot me, be sure to make a note of the secret codeword I'm holding.
The codeword unlocks a secret level of the amazing Gargoylz game on our fabulous website at
www.gargolyz.co.uk

Oldacre Primary School

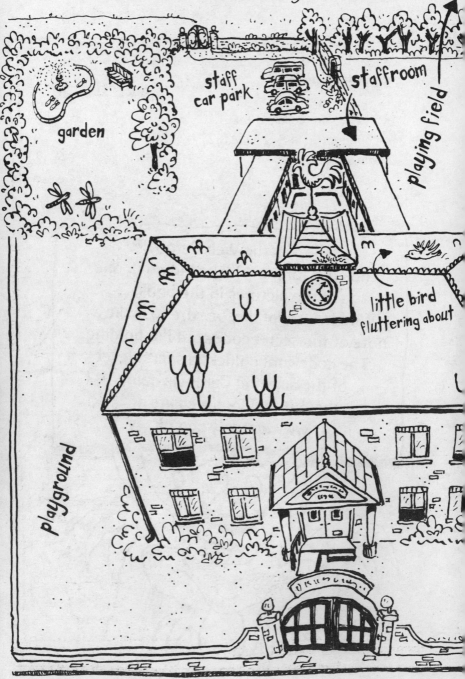

St Mark's Church

playground

School Report - Max Black

Days absent: 0

Days late: 0

Max is a bright boy. If he spent as much time on his school work as he does on annoying Lucinda Tellingly he would get much better marks. I am pleased to see that he enjoys exercise - although I do not count running down corridors making racing car noises. Also I would be glad if he did not shout "Awesome" quite so loudly every time we have football practice.

Class teacher - Miss Deirdre Bleet

The only good thing I can say about Max Black is that he is always early for school. However, he is the last one into the classroom. He spends far too much time playing tricks with Ben Neal. Mrs Pumpkin is still off sick after discovering an earwig farm in her handbag. Max ignores all school rules. He has recently developed a curious interest in drainpipes and has been seen talking to the wall. This behaviour is outrageous and must stop.

Head teacher - Hagatha Hogsbottom (Mrs)

School Report - Ben Neal

Days absent: 0

Days late: 0

Ben has many abilities which he does not always use. He works very hard at dreaming up tricks to play, which gives him very little time to concentrate on his learning. He enjoys football and skateboarding - indeed, he and his board can frequently be found upside down in a flowerbed.

Class teacher - Miss Deirdre Bleet

Ben Neal is a strange boy. He is often to be found grinning at gutters.
He constantly breaks school rule number 742: boys must not break school rules.
Ben thinks he can get away with anything by flashing his blue eyes and looking innocent. I am not fooled.
Indeed I am still waiting for him and Max Black to write a note of apology to Mr Bucket the caretaker. Gluing his wellington boots to the staffroom ceiling was outrageous!

Head teacher - Hagatha Hogsbottom (Mrs)

Contents

1. Toby Turns Up   1

2. The Big Stink   31

3. Spider Surprise   61

4. Now You See It, Now You Don't!   89

1. Toby Turns Up

Max Black zoomed out of his front door. He was playing his usual game on the way to school. He was a nine-year-old secret agent, speeding along in his super powered spy plane.

"MAX!"

He skidded to a halt, trainers smoking. His mum was standing in the front garden.

"You've forgotten your school bag again!" she called, holding it out.

Max ran back and snatched it up.

"Did you brush your hair this morning?" demanded his mother.

"Yes, Mum." Of course he hadn't. He'd lost his brush down the toilet months ago. His dark brown hair stuck up all over the place and that was how he liked it.

Max set off along the pavement again. There was a boy ahead of him dribbling a football. Max activated his spy radar to check him out: blond hair, blue eyes, big grin, nine and a quarter years old.

He knew what that meant. It was Ben Neal, codename: Best Friend.

Max sneaked up behind him. "Agent Black ready for action," he hissed in Ben's ear.

Ben grinned and passed the ball to Max's feet. "New spy mission," he yelled, running ahead. "Get football to school at top speed."

They were soon at the gates. Max looked up at Oldacre Primary School, sandwiched between the ancient stone church and the post office.

"Another day of torture," he groaned.

"Bell's not rung yet," said Ben. "Let's practise some nifty football skills."

"You're on," said Max as they ran through the playground. His spy radar homed in on someone: pale, skinny, face like a weasel. Max knew what that meant. It was Enemy Agent Lucinda Tellingly, codename: Bossy Boots. "Bet you can't lob the ball right over Lucinda's head."

SPY FILE:

codename:
Bossy Boots

"That'll be hard," said Ben. "She's got the biggest head in the world!"

Lucinda was standing near the netball hoop. Ben placed the ball carefully on the ground and took three steps back.

"Watch," he said. "Straight over her head and through the hoop."

Wham! Up went the ball. Down it came – **thump!** – right on top of Lucinda's ponytail. It bounced off sideways and landed on the low flat roof over the staffroom.

"Now look what you've done, Lucinda," moaned Ben, peering up at the ball. "It's stuck."

"Good!" snapped Lucinda. "I hope you never get it back." Lucinda didn't like Max and Ben – the boys had no idea why.

Just then, the bell rang for the beginning of school and Lucinda stomped off, tidying her ponytail.

"How am I going to get my ball down?" sighed Ben, ignoring the bell.

"We could try a fishing rod with glue on the end," suggested Max.

Ben's eyes lit up. "Brilliant plan, Agent Black." Then he frowned. "There's just one tiny problem – we don't have a fishing rod."

"Then we'll have to get onto the roof," said Max. "And I know how. We'll climb

up on that skip in the teachers' car park."

The skip was full of old furniture. Using a bookcase as a ladder, the boys were soon up on the staffroom roof.

Suddenly there was a skittering, scrabbling noise behind them. They whirled round.

Their eyes nearly popped out of their heads. A very peculiar creature was bounding towards them. It was the size of a puppy and it scampered along on all four paws. It had a monkey face with long pointy ears and golden eyes that glinted in the sunshine. Its skin looked exactly like the stone on the church next door.

Leafy wings sprouted from its back and its dragon-like tail wagged merrily.

The creature skidded to a halt, squatted on its hind legs and gave Max and Ben a huge grin.

"I think it's a gargoyle!" whispered Max.

"Do you mean one of those stone things on the church?" asked Ben.

"Yes," said Max. "They hang under the gutters and spout rainwater."

"But it can't be a gargoyle," Ben objected. "Gargoyles are just statues. They're not alive."

"This one is," said Max, staring.

"Greetingz," said the gargoyle merrily. His voice was a mixture between a growl and a purr – like a sort of dog-cat. "I'm Tobias the Third. You can call me Toby. I live on the church porch." He put his head on one side and peered at them. "Spluttering gutterz!" he chortled. "Are you school gargoylz? You're the ugliest ones I've ever seen."

"We're not gargoyles," Max told him.

Toby's impish face creased up in a frown. "Of course you're gargoylz!" he said. "You were climbing on the roof and making mischief. Only gargoylz do that." He gave Max's arm a pinch. "Your stone is a bit flabby though."

"We're not made of stone," Ben explained.

"We're boys. I'm Ben and this is Max."

Toby looked horrified. "You mean you're humanz? But humanz aren't supposed to know that gargoylz are alive!

What am I going to do?" He began to wail and bite his claws.

"We won't tell anyone about you," Max shouted above the noise. "We promise, don't we, Ben?"

"I promise never to tell a soul that gargoylz are alive," Ben said solemnly. He picked up his football. "Cross my heart and may I never play with this again if I do."

Toby perked up immediately. "Glad we got that sorted out," he purred.

A booming voice suddenly rose from below. "What are you boys doing?"

Toby looked startled. "Freeze!" he whispered. He squatted on his haunches, put on a frozen, wide-mouthed snarl and kept absolutely still. Now he looked just like the gargoyles on the church.

Max peered cautiously over the guttering. He activated his spy radar: grey hair, beaky nose, steam coming out of ears. He knew what that meant.

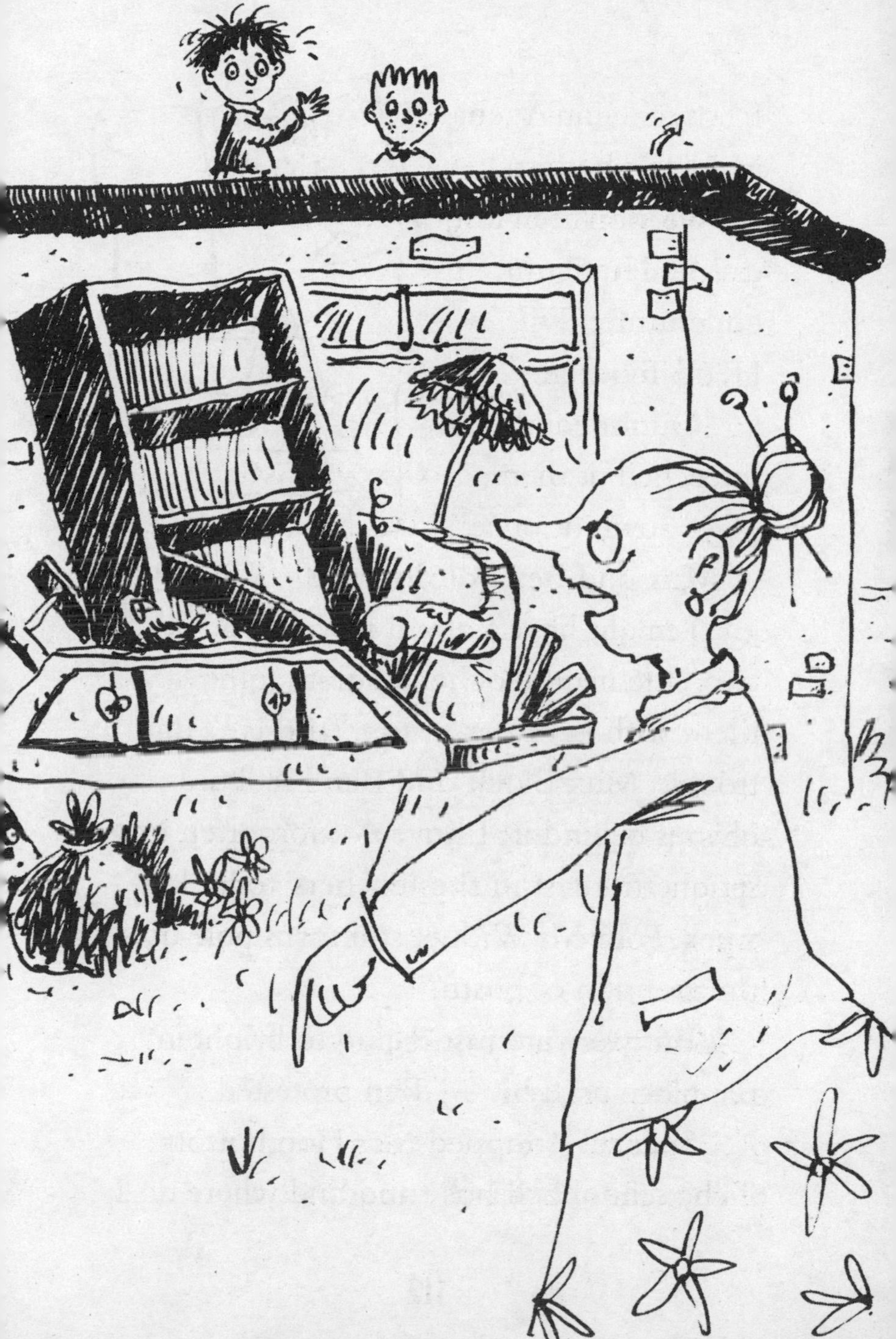

It was Enemy Agent Mrs Hogsbottom, commonly known as Mrs Hogsbum, codename: Evil Head Teacher.

"Outrageous!" she screeched at them. "Get down at once!"

Max and Ben got down.

"I might have known it would be you two," the head teacher said, studying them with her laser vision. "If there's any trouble, Max Black and Ben Neal are always behind it! I have not forgotten your spaghetti forest in the teachers' toilet last week. Poor Mr Widget still turns pale at the mention of pasta."

"But we were just trying to brighten the place up a bit—" Ben protested.

"Silence!" snapped Mrs Hogsbottom. "The school bell has rung and where do I find you? Running about on the roof."

"We weren't running, miss," Max tried to explain. "We—"

"No arguing!" ordered Mrs Hogsbottom fiercely. "School rule number fifty-six: children must not argue."

Ben put on his special wide-eyed innocent face. It always worked on the dinner ladies, who gave him extra sausages. It never worked on Mrs Hogsbum. Her bony fingers shot out and snatched the football from him.

"But—" began Max.

"Get to your classroom at once!" snapped the head teacher.

"When can I have my—?" began Ben.

"You can have your football back at the end of the week," snarled Mrs Hogsbum as she stormed off, "and not before!"

"How ungrateful!" fumed Max. "Especially when we saved the caretaker all the trouble of having to fetch it for us." He looked up at the roof. "Toby? Are you still there?"

There was a scrabbling sound and then the gargoyle's chirpy little face appeared over the edge of the gutter. "Glad that ugly monster's gone," he said.

"She's worse than a monster," Max told him. "Monsters run away when they see *her*."

"And now she's got my football," grumbled Ben. "I bet that's the last I'll see of it."

"She might burst it with her horrible

sharp nose," said Max. "Or flatten it under a pile of maths books,"

said Ben. "Or cut it into tiny pieces and boil it up in her cauldron," Max added. "I know what will cheer you up," grinned Toby. "I'll show you how I can fly. It's my special power."

"Awesome!" said Ben, football forgotten.

But before Toby could move, Mrs Hogsbottom's head

popped out of the staffroom window like a fearsome jack-in-the-box. "Off to class!" she bellowed. "IMMEDIATELY!"

The boys scampered for the door. Max looked back to wave at Toby, but the gargoyle had gone.

"Did you see Toby's wings?" whispered Max as he and Ben bent over their class maths test. "I can't wait to see him fly."

"And he talked about making mischief," said Ben. "He's our sort of gargoyle!"

"I've just had a brilliant idea," declared Max. "We must get to the girls' loo – now."

Ben looked horrified. "You call that a brilliant idea? I wouldn't be seen dead in that stinky place. It's all clean and flowery!"

"True," Max agreed. "But if you look out of one of the windows up there, you can see the staffroom roof. We might spot Toby again."

"Good thinking, Agent Black," said Ben.

"That *is* a brilliant idea. There's just one problem — we need to come up with a way to get out of here."

"Max and Ben!" snapped a voice behind them.

Max's spy radar told him what that meant: short and dumpy, limp brown hair, silly half-moon glasses. It was Enemy Agent Miss Bleet, codename: Wimpy Teacher.

"Wasting time chatting, are we?" sighed Miss Bleet. She always sounded tired when she spoke to Max and Ben. Max thought she should go to bed earlier. "Ben, go and sit with Poppy," she went on. "Max, stay where you are. Then you might both do some work."

"See you in the girls' loos," Max hissed as Ben

pushed his
chair back noisily.
Max chewed his
pencil. He was just
wondering how to escape
when a paper aeroplane
sailed past Miss Bleet, who nearly fell into
the wastepaper bin in fright. The missile
banked and turned and hit Max on the
ear. He picked it up. It was Ben's maths
test – beautifully folded.

"Ben Neal!" quavered their teacher.
"Go and stand outside in the corridor."

Max was impressed. Who'd have
thought that a boring test
could be so useful? It had
got Ben out of class. Now
it was his turn to escape.
He stuck up his hand.

"Can I go to the toilet
please, miss?"

"You'll have to wait till playtime," Miss Bleet said, looking impatient.

Right, thought Max, *time for Secret Plan: Bursting.* He crossed his legs and bounced up and down on his seat. "Oooh, miss!" he groaned.

But for once Miss Bleet wasn't budging.

Time for Secret Plan: Explosion, Max thought. He held his breath and crossed his eyes.

"He's going to wet himself!" squealed Lucinda.

Max let out a terrible moaning sound. Lucinda shrieked, and Tiffany and Shannon moved their chairs away. Everyone in the class craned their necks to watch.

"OK, you can go," said Miss Bleet hurriedly. "But come straight back."

Max was out of the classroom before she could say homework. He sprinted down the empty corridor, leaped up the

stairs two at a time and burst into the
girls' toilets.

Ben's head peeped out of one of the
cubicles. He beckoned to Max. "I've found
the right window."

Max squeezed in and pushed the door
shut behind him. There was a small open
window above the toilet.

Ben climbed on the seat. "Get up here,"
he said. "It's a great view. But the seat's a
bit dodgy."

Max scrambled up next to him and they
clung to the window ledge, peering out.

"ROOAARR!"

A terrifying, snarling face appeared at the window right in front of them.

"Yow!" cried Max, jumping backwards and knocking into Ben.

CRACK!

The toilet seat broke off its hinges and the two boys tumbled to the floor.

Max sat up. Ben was sitting next to him, the toilet seat round his neck. Max could hear chortling. He looked up at the window to see Toby sticking

his tongue out at them, his golden eyes shining with mischief.

Suddenly the cubicle door burst open. Toby ducked out of sight.

"Max Black and Ben Neal!" exclaimed Miss Bleet. "What are you doing in the girls' lavatories? And *why* are you wearing a toilet seat, Ben?"

"I'm not wearing it, miss," began Ben dizzily. "I was just—"

"I don't want to hear any excuses," sighed Miss Bleet. "You can both spend playtime *and* lunch time tidying the stock cupboard."

"Boring," grumbled Max as they trailed back to class. "Bet she won't let us run beetle races or stick crayons up our noses like we did last time."

"And we won't be able to see Toby again till after school!" added Ben miserably.

For the rest of the day Max and Ben did everything they could to get out of the classroom, but nothing worked – not even when Max told Miss Bleet he'd been bitten by a super-poisonous spider and needed to go to the nurse.

When the bell went, they were first through the door.

"Can you see Toby?" yelled Max as they ran into the playground.

"Not a claw in sight," answered Ben.

Max stopped. A horrible thought had hit him. "Do you think he's gone for good?"

Ben shook his head. "Can't have. He's probably back home on the church."

"Good thinking, Agent Neal," said Max. "Let's search there."

They ran into the churchyard.

"There he is!" shouted Ben, pointing up at the porch. "But he's not moving."

The little monkey-like stone creature was hanging just under the guttering, his mouth in a wide, fixed snarl.

"Hey, Toby," called Max. "Remember us?"

The stone eyes didn't blink. They just stared blankly over the churchyard.

"What's wrong with him?" asked Ben.
A look of horror came over his face. "We
didn't imagine it, did we?"

"No," Max hissed, pointing. "That's the
answer. He's seen Mrs Hogsbum coming."

Their head teacher was steaming down
the path towards them.

"What are you doing here?" she
demanded. "Have you lost a football on
the church roof? School rule number one
hundred and thirty-three: boys must not
lose footballs on the church roof."

The boys shook their heads.

"HURUMPH!" Mrs Hogsbottom
glared suspiciously at the guttering.

There was a very rude noise and a
whoosh, and suddenly a flood of dirty
rainwater spewed from Toby's open
mouth straight into the head teacher's face.

Max and Ben burst out laughing.
Mrs Hogsbum's grey hair was plastered
to her head like a swimming cap.

A tangle of leaves and old pine cones
was stuck over one ear and her mascara
had run. She looked like a
demented zebra.

"Outrageous!" she spluttered as she squelched back to school. "Go home this instant!"

Toby launched himself off the gutter and zoomed around the boys' heads, doing victory loop-the-loops.

"Spluttering gutterz!" he yelled as he went. "That's the best trick I've done since I dropped a slug on the vicar's head in the middle of a wedding."

"It was awesome," laughed Max. "And you can really fly! That's awesome too!"

"*Totally* awesome!" agreed Ben, watching Toby swooping up and down in glee.

Toby waved merrily. "Got to go. See you!" And, with that, he flew over the church tower and out of sight.

"I never thought I'd say this," said Ben, "but I'm really looking forward to school tomorrow."

"Me too." Max grinned. "We're going to have the best fun ever now that Toby's our friend!"

2. The Big Stink

Max and Ben zoomed along the road on Ben's skateboard. Today they were secret agents working undercover as racing drivers. They swerved in through the school gates, hit a dustbin and fell off into a bush.

"Record speed in the World Championships!" exclaimed Max, brushing twigs out of his hair.

"Cool spin at the last bend," agreed Ben as he inspected his skateboard for damage.

Max glanced around the playground and dropped his voice like a good spy. "Today's mission – find Toby!" He looked eagerly over the school wall at the church porch, where their new gargoyle friend lived. "I wonder what tricks he'll play today."

"Out of my way!" came a harsh voice.

Max activated his spy radar: shaved head, big fists, evil scowl. He knew what that meant. It was Enemy Agent Barry Price, also known as The Basher, codename: School Bully.

Barry stomped around with a nasty smirk on his face. Some reception kids were standing in a line, taking it in turns

to play hopscotch — at least they were until
The Basher bashed into them. They fell
down like skittles.

"Hide!" whispered Max. "We don't
want to be next."

The boys ducked down behind the
dustbins.

There was an evil glint in The Basher's
eye as he marched towards some girls who

were skipping, but
before he could reach
them, he leaped
into the air with a
shriek, clutching
his bottom. An
acorn fell to the
ground and rolled away.
Barry spotted the acorn
and snatched it up. "Who
threw that?" he snarled.
Max and Ben had
to stifle their giggles as another acorn
hit The Basher on the nose. There was a
wheezy sniggering sound above them.
Max's spy radar snapped into action:
monkey face, big pointy ears, wicked grin.
He knew what that meant. It was Toby,
their gargoyle friend. He was peering
down from the church roof – and he had a
catapult in his paw.

"Hi, Toby!" yelled Max. They ran over

to the wall by the churchyard.

"Greetingz," the gargoyle called in his growly purr. "Can't stop. Bit busy."

Whizz! Ping! Whoosh! He fired off a barrage of acorns. The Basher leaped like a jumping bean all over the playground as the mini missiles bounced off him. At last he fled round the corner.

"So you were the one firing at The Basher!" said Ben, impressed. "Serves that bully right."

"We got rid of him!" said a timid voice

from the roof. The boys could just see
a pair of rabbitty ears sticking up
behind Toby.

"Hey, Toby," Max called. "Who's that?"

"This is Barnabas," announced Toby.
"He lives on the church tower. He's my
friend." He beckoned with a claw. "Come
and say hello, Barney."

The new gargoyle slowly waddled to
the edge of the roof. He had a face like
a soppy dog, with round, solemn eyes. All

down his back was a ridge of spikes that reminded Max of a stegosaurus.

Barney took one look at Max and Ben and began to shake like a jelly. "Humanz!" he whimpered. "But humanz aren't supposed to know that gargoylz are alive. What are we going to do?" He froze, his eyes glazed and a terrible pong filled the air.

"**PHWOAAHH!**" gasped Max, holding his nose. "What's that?"

"Smells like the stinkiest stink bomb *ever!*" spluttered Ben, backing away.

"Smellz is Barney's special power," said Toby. "Just like mine's flying."

"And drenching head teachers!" added Max.

"All gargoylz can empty gutterz from their mouths," said Toby. "That's easy – but when Barney does a bottom burp, everybody runs." He cupped his paw to his mouth so that only the boys could hear. "Trouble is, sometimes he gets nervous and makes the smell by accident."

"It's an awesome power," said Max. "I wish I could do it. Don't be scared of us, Barney. We won't tell anyone about you."

Barney twitched an ear and slowly came back to life.

"This is Max and Ben," explained Toby. "They're full of tricks, just like us gargoylz."

"Pleased to meet you," whispered Barney. He wrinkled his nose and sniffed the air like a dog. "What's that delightful smell?"

"Doesn't he know it stinks?" gasped Ben in amazement.

But the gargoylz weren't listening.

"I can smell it too," said Toby, his golden eyes shining. "It's *wonderful!*"

"It's coming from that funny-looking human with her tail on her head," said Barney. "You didn't tell me humanz could make smellz like that."

Puzzled, Ben and Max sniffed. As Barney's pong faded away, they got a wonderful whiff of warm, freshly baked cookie.

Max gazed longingly in the direction of the smell. Someone was clutching a cake tin. His spy radar went mad: pale, skinny, face like a weasel. Max knew what that meant. It was Enemy Agent Lucinda Tellingly.

"Lucinda's been baking," gasped Max.

"Happy birthday, Poppy," they heard her say in her shrill voice. "I made these specially. The biggest one's for you."

"What a creep," muttered Max.

"Those cookies look awesome though," said Ben. "I want one."

Lucinda was passing the tin around to her friends. "Help yourselves," she said smugly.

Max winked at Ben and grinned.
"Don't mind if I do!" He leaped onto
the skateboard
and sped across
towards the girls.
As he passed
by, he snatched
a cookie from
the tin.

"I'll get you for
that, Max Black,"
Lucinda yelled
after him. "You
wait!"

"I was just helping
myself like you said," Max called back,
expertly flipping the skateboard to a stop
by the wall.

The cookie was still warm and bursting
with gooey chocolate chips. Max saw
three pairs of eyes on him. He sighed and
broke it into four pieces.

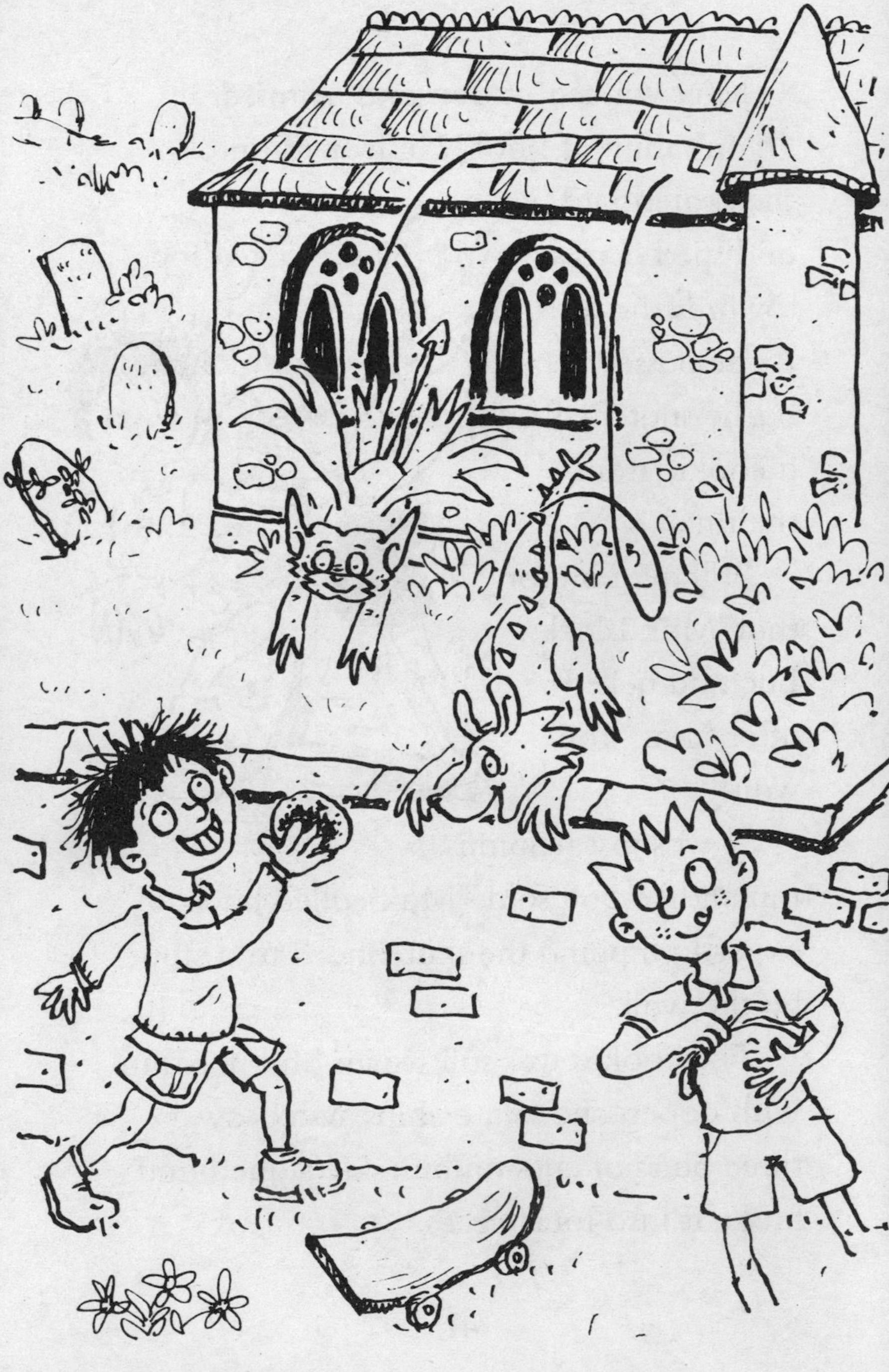

Toby and Barney jumped down from the church roof onto the wall. They grabbed a piece each.

"What do we do with them?" asked Toby.

"I'll show you." Ben laughed and gobbled his chunk of cookie down in one gulp. "I don't care what Lucinda does to us after this," he sighed, rubbing his tummy. "It was worth it."

Toby and Barney looked at each other, then stuffed their pieces of cookie in their mouths like Ben. Huge smiles spread across their stone faces.

"Nice," said Toby.

"Nice?" gasped Barney, chocolate smeared all over his doggy nose. "It's *delicious*!"

Just then the bell rang. Max heard heavy footsteps behind him. He turned. It was Mrs Hogsbum.

Toby and Barney froze right there on the wall, faces covered in chocolate.

As usual Mrs Hogsbottom made a

beeline for the boys.
"School rule number
two hundred and
twenty-seven,"
she began.
"Boys must
not stand next
to walls and
look innocent
when—" She
stopped and

gawped at the unexpected stone figures on
the wall.

"Are you all right, miss?" asked Max.

"Did you put those . . . things . . . there?"
demanded Mrs Hogsbottom, turning to
stare at the two boys.

As she turned, Toby and Barney
disappeared behind the wall.

Ben opened his eyes wide and
attempted to look innocent. "What things,
miss?" he asked sweetly.

Mrs Hogsbottom looked back at
the now-empty wall. Her eyes bulged.
"Outrageous!" she spluttered.

"I think you need to sit down, miss,"
said Max kindly. "You're not getting any
younger. We'll take you inside."

"See you," Max heard faintly as he and
Ben led their gibbering
head teacher away.

★ ★ ★

Toby and Barney didn't reappear at
playtime or lunch time.

"There's not even a whiff of a pong,"
moaned Max as they went in for
afternoon lessons.

"It's been such a boring morning,"
complained Ben. "Miss Bleet even stopped
us doing our woodlouse Olympics up and
down the table."

"She wouldn't listen when I said they
needed their exercise," added Max sadly.

"Shame Lucinda didn't try and get
revenge for the cookie-theft," said Ben. "At
least that might have been interesting."

"I expect she's chickened out,"
answered Max.

"Hey, I've just remembered," said
Ben, cheering up suddenly. "We've got
football now."

Max brightened too and the boys sped
into the cloakroom to change, leaving their

clothes in the usual messy pile on the floor.

"Last one on the field is a banana!" yelled Max as they burst into the corridor and dodged one of the girls.

"Out of the way, Lucinda!"

"That was a great match," said Max, admiring the mud splodges on his arms.

"We only lost by one goal." He and Ben bounded into the boys' cloakroom.

"What's that smell?" gasped Ben, staggering backwards. "It's . . ."

"Sweet . . ." said Max.

"Flowery . . ." added Ben.

"Hideous!" shuddered Max, flapping his hand in front of his nose.

Duncan laughed. "And it's coming from *your clothes*," he told them.

Max and Ben picked up their uniforms. All the boys were laughing now.

"They stink!" wailed Ben. "Someone's put perfume all over them."

"Yeeuurgh!" said Max, looking furious. "I bet I know who did it . . ."

"Lucinda Tellingly!" the boys cried together.

"She's got her revenge – we can't wear our uniforms like this," said Ben in disgust.

"We could keep our football kit on instead," suggested Max.

"Miss Bleet would have a fit if we did that!" Ben said.

Then he grinned. "It might be fun."

"But then she'd ban us from football for a month," Max pointed out. He held his nose and started pulling on his uniform. Ben groaned and did the same.

They made their way back to the classroom, leaving a trail of flowery pong behind them. As they came in, the whole class turned to see what the smell was.

A wave of laughter rippled round the
room and Max noticed that Lucinda had
a smug smile on her face.

"This is war!" he muttered to her. He
slid into his seat and hunched down, trying
to be invisible.

"Quiet now, please," called Miss Bleet.
She beamed at the class. "I hope you've all
remembered to study your lines."

There were eager nods all round.

"Oh, no," whispered Ben. "It's drama
and I didn't learn my words for that stupid
play she wrote about pixies."

"Me neither," said Max. "Miss Bleet's
going to be furious . . . No, wait a minute,
I've just had a fantastic idea! I know
how to get us out of trouble *and* have our
revenge on Lucinda at the same time!"
He started rummaging in his rucksack.
"Thought so," he said after a moment.
"I've still got Old
Pongo!" He
showed Ben a
small round ball.

"A stink bomb!"
Ben was delighted.
"Good plan. She
stank *us* out, so

we'll do the same to her."

"Watch this." Max rolled the ball expertly under Lucinda's chair. "She's bound to step on it, and Miss Bleet won't bother about *us* when she gets a whiff of Old Pongo."

Soon it was Lucinda's turn to say her lines. She was Chief Pixie. She pushed her chair back to stand up. The stink bomb was right under her foot. Any minute now . . .

"What's that?" asked their teacher suddenly. Just as Lucinda's foot came down, Miss Bleet fished the ball out from under it. She frowned at it suspiciously, then plonked it on her table. Lucinda flung out a dramatic arm and began.

"We've had it," Max groaned to Ben as the Chief Pixie squeaked through her lines.

"Things can't get any worse. We smell like a flower shop *and* we're going to get into mega trouble for not knowing our lines."

But Ben wasn't listening. He was pointing to Lucinda's bag, which lay at her feet. Max looked down. A cheeky monkey face was poking out of it.

"Toby!" Max gasped under his breath. Their small friend waved merrily at them.

"And Barney!" whispered Ben as the little gargoyle popped up next to Toby.

"Barney with the special power of a *stink bomb*!" Max's eyes lit up. "We're not going to get into trouble after all – as long as I can get Barney to understand that we need one of his really strong pongs."

Max held his nose and pulled a revolting face at Barney, as if he could

smell something awful, but shy Barney
went bright red and covered his eyes.
Max decided to see if he could get Toby
to understand instead. Then *he* could
explain to Barney. He pulled a face at Toby.

Toby pulled a face back.

"It's not a game," Max muttered to
himself. "We need a stinker." Lucinda had
almost finished and it was his turn next!

He held his nose, flapped his hand
in the air in desperation and pointed at

Barney. A grin slowly spread over Toby's face. He grabbed his friend by one ear and whispered into it. After a moment Barney nodded enthusiastically, then his eyes glazed and a few seconds later an appalling smell rose from underneath Lucinda's chair. Toby and Barney ducked speedily out of sight, sniggering.

The class leaped to their feet, coughing and spluttering. Duncan put his PE bag over his head.

"Lucinda . . ." croaked Miss Bleet, clamping a hankie over her face as her eyes started to water.

"It wasn't me, miss!" said Lucinda indignantly. She glared at Max and Ben. "I bet it was—"

But Miss Bleet wasn't listening.

"Everybody out!" she ordered, shooing the class towards the door. "Make for the playground."

"It's like fire drill," said Max in delight.

"Stink drill!" Ben laughed.

There was a rush for the door. Lucinda was at the front of the queue.

Soon everyone had gone.

Toby and Barney popped out of their hiding place and perched on Miss Bleet's table. Holding their noses, the boys dashed over to them.

"That was great!" Ben told the gargoylz. Toby grinned. "Barney's best trick since  he stank out the vicar's Christmas party," he said.

Barney grinned too.

"But what were you doing in Lucinda's bag anyway?" asked Max.

Toby and Barney looked a bit sheepish.

"We were on a cookie hunt," explained Toby. "That one this morning was so scrumptious."

"But we couldn't find any," put in Barney, looking disappointed.

"You deserve all the cookies you can get your paws on!" exclaimed Max, finding it was safe to stop holding his nose.

"It's thanks to you we're not in trouble," added Ben. "And everyone thinks Lucinda made the stink! We win all round."

Barney bounced up and down on the table in excitement.

"No, Barney!" yelled Toby.

But it was too late. Another dreadful stench was filling the air.

"I forgot to say," said Toby, scooting off to the window. "Barney makes stinks when he's excited as well."

"Uh-oh!" yelled Max and Ben. "Wait for us!"

3. Spider Surprise

DER-RING!

"Answer the door, please," yelled Max's mum from upstairs.

Secret Agent Max Black threw open the front door and aimed his super spy-zapper at the intruder. Ben stood there, dangling a huge hairy spider in front of Max's nose.

"Awesome, Agent Neal!" breathed Max.

"His name's Sidney," Ben told him. "He looks real, doesn't he? I put him on my mum's cornflakes at breakfast. I thought she'd never come down from the ceiling. Then Arabella ruined it by telling her it was a toy. Sisters!"

Max caught sight of something at the top of the stairs. He activated his spy radar: small, shriekingly loud and extremely annoying. He knew what that meant. It was Enemy Agent Jessica Black, codename: Disgusting Little

Codename: Disgusting Little Sister

SPY FILE:

Sister. She was in the middle of brushing her teeth and she leaned over the banister to pull an ugly, foamy face at them. Then she darted back to the bathroom.

"Can I test Sidney out before we go off to school?" Max asked Ben.

His sister's coat was hanging invitingly on a hook near the door.

"Be my guest." Ben grinned as he

handed the spider over.

Carefully Max wedged Sidney in the cuff of the coat. Little rubber pads on the ends of the spider's legs made it nice and sticky.

Soon Jessica came pounding down the stairs, pushing past the boys. She stuck out her tongue at them and grabbed her coat. Max and Ben stood back and waited.

"**AAAARRRGHHHH!**"

"I'll save you, Jess," yelled Max over the ear-splitting screech.

He dived forward, knocked Jessica off
her feet, snatched the spider and dashed
out of the front door. Ben followed close
behind. They skidded down the path and
hid behind a bush.

"I didn't want Mum seeing Sidney,"
Max explained, handing the spider back to
Ben. "And now I'll be a hero for rescuing
Jessica from the monster. She won't pull
faces at me again in a hurry."

"You think you've got it bad," said
Ben. "Older sisters are worse. You should
try Arabella. Mrs Hogsbum's made her a
monitor at school and the power's gone to
her head."

"That's dreadful!" said Max. "Better keep away from her."

Max and Ben strolled into the bustling playground.

"Let's do the spider trick again," said Ben, "before school starts." He looked around. "Who's going to scream the loudest?"

Max scanned the playground, spy radar active. He soon spotted something: clean uniforms, pink ribbons, girly giggling. He knew what that meant. Three enemy agents: Lucinda Tellingly, Poppy Parker and Tiffany Goodchild.

"I can see some likely screamers," he said. "On the bench over there."

"Brilliant," said Ben. "Tiffany's put her bag down. It's just waiting for a nice, fat, juicy spider."

Whistling innocently, the boys ambled past Tiffany and her chums. At just the right moment, Ben let Sidney fall.

"Bull's-eye!" muttered Max as the spider landed right on top of her bag.

The boys raced off to their favourite hiding place behind the bushes, and settled down to wait for the action.

"AAARRRGHHH!"

The ear-piercing screams of Lucinda, Poppy and Tiffany could be heard all over the school. The boys high-fived.

"My turn to be the hero," said Ben.
"I must rescue the poor girlies from the
horrible spider." He sprinted across the
playground, Max on his tail, and nearly
crashed into Miss Bleet.

"Looking for this?"
she asked, holding out
the spider between
two trembling
fingers. "I just
knew it would have
something to do with
you two. You can have

it back at lunch time. And you will be on
late lunch because you will be doing a
little job for me first."

"But it's chocolate pudding today," wailed Max. "There won't be any left by late lunch."

"Well, you can think about that while everyone else is eating and you are taking letters round to all the classrooms," said Miss Bleet. She scurried off towards the staffroom, holding the spider at arm's length.

"Teachers and girls are all the same," moaned Max. "No sense of humour."

"Greetingz!" came a growly purr from above.

The boys looked up in delight. It was Toby, their gargoyle friend. He had a huge smile on his monkey-like face and he was hanging upside down from the gutter of the roof.

"Why so grumpy?" he asked. "What's the matter?"

"Miss Bleet has taken Sidney, my
super-scary, hairy spider," said Ben,
pointing crossly at his teacher.

"What a mean thing to do!" said Toby.
"Don't worry – I'll get it back." And he
scampered away across the roof.

★ ★ ★

At playtime Max and Ben dashed outside.

"I hope Toby got Sidney back," said Max, scanning all the gutters for the gargoyle. "We've already missed out on two lessons worth of spider mischief."

"There he is," yelled Ben, pointing at the kitchen roof. "And he's got another gargoyle with him. It's one we haven't met before."

They sprinted across to the kitchen.

"I couldn't find your spider, Ben," said Toby, "even though I turned out your teacher's whole desk! This is Bartholomew, by the way."

Bartholomew was smaller than Toby, with wide, bulging cheeks and pointed ears. He had a big round belly and wore a pleated skirt like a gladiator. He had a grumpy expression on  his face. He took one look at the boys and began to complain.

"These are humanz, Toby," he growled in a gurgly voice. "They're not meant to know we're alive."

"I told you about them, Bart," said Toby. "They won't give away our secret. Don't be such a grouch." He turned back to the boys. "As I couldn't find your spider, I brought Bart along instead."

"But Bart doesn't look anything *like* a spider!" said Max.

Toby guffawed. "Of course he doesn't.

But wait till you see his special power. Go on, Bart."

Muttering to himself, Bart clambered down the drainpipe and squatted on the ground. Then he opened his mouth wide and . . . burped! It was an enormous burp, and as it ended a huge, furry black spider dropped out of Bart's mouth and scuttled away across the playground.

"Wow!" exclaimed Max.

"Is it real?" gasped Ben.

The spider suddenly vanished into thin air.

"Course it's not real," Bart told them.

"My spiders don't last long and they don't hurt anybody, but they *look* real."

"That's so cool," said Max in admiration.

"And perfect for playing tricks," added Ben.

Bart stopped looking grumpy and grinned. "My record is a ten-minute tarantula," he told them.

"Could you burp up some spiders for us to take into class?" Max asked.

"My pleasure," said Bart.

Max rummaged in his rucksack and found a plastic pot. He chucked out the mouldy raisins inside and held the pot out to Bart.

Burrrrp! Arrrp! Barump!

Three hairy spiders fell into Max's pot. He put the lid on quickly.

"Thanks, Bart," he said, impressed. "We're going to have some fun with these."

Just then the bell went. Mrs Hogsbottom, the head teacher, looked very surprised to see Max and Ben running into class first.

Max waited until everyone was sitting quietly. He was on the same table as Poppy. He reached into his bag and pulled out the pot. Slowly he prised open the lid and started to tip his spiders out onto Poppy's English book . . . But nothing

happened. He'd waited too long. The
spiders had gone.

At lunch time Max and Ben tried to sneak
out before Miss Bleet could give them
their punishment. But their teacher was
standing in the doorway with a pile of
papers in her hands.

"I want you to put one of these letters on every pupil's desk. It's all about a lovely trip to a sewing-machine museum." She took Sidney out of her pocket. "And you can have this back," she added. "But no more frightening Tiffany."

"We won't, miss," promised Max and Ben as they set off round the school.

"I've got a great idea," said Max when they got to the first classroom. "We don't have to go round putting a letter on every desk. Watch my incredible skill. In one clever throw I will place a letter on each chair."

76

He took a handful of letters
and hurled them through
the doorway. The letters
fluttered about and floated
down to land on a few chairs
– and all over the floor.

"That was quick," Ben
said happily. "At this rate
there'll still be loads of
choccy pudding left."
Five minutes later
every classroom
was covered in paper
and Max and Ben were
standing eagerly in the
dinner queue.

Ben took Sidney out of his pocket. "Time for a bit of fun after all that hard work," he whispered. "We only promised not to frighten *Tiffany*. Let's try Sidney out on Duncan."

Duncan was standing in front of them. Ben put the spider on his shoulder. "Excuse  me," he said politely, "but is that a tarantula?"

Duncan looked down and saw the huge spider. "Get it off me!" he yelped, flailing about and swatting madly at Sidney.

"What's going on?" came a sharp voice.

Max looked up, his spy radar on alert: pigtails bobbing, monitor's badge gleaming, smug smile all over her face. He knew what that meant. It was Enemy Agent Arabella Neal, Ben's sister, codename: Manic Monitor.

"Oh, Ben," she said in a mock sad voice, peeling Sidney off Duncan's quivering back. "You're not still playing with that silly toy, are you? It doesn't even look real."

"Yes it *does*!" insisted Ben. "Duncan thought so."

"*I'm* the monitor here," said Arabella, sticking her nose in his face, "and it's what *I* think that counts." She smiled evilly. "I'm keeping this stupid spider and you two can go to the back of the queue."

"But that's not fair!" exclaimed Max.

"Tough!" Arabella stalked off, holding Sidney by one leg.

Max and Ben slunk to the end of the line. "They're sure to run out of chocolate pudding now," moaned Max.

"And we've lost Sidney again," said Ben, watching his sister march away.

"But that's not the worst thing," Max went on gloomily. "The worst thing is that now we'll have to eat with the monitors, because they always eat last."

"And *that* means Arabella!" groaned Ben.

Suddenly Max's face lit up. "I have a cunning plan!" he cried, and dashed away.

He got back just as Ben was being served.

"There's only one chocolate pudding left," sighed Ben.

"I don't mind," said Max. "We can share. We're going to have some fun, Agent Neal. Our mission is to sit by a window as close to Arabella as we can get."

"You're joking!" exclaimed Ben. "She'll boss us to death."

"But my plan depends on it," insisted Max.

Ben nodded, picked up his tray and zoomed across the dining hall to the table next to his sister.

Max plonked himself down beside him. "I've had a word with some *friends*," he murmured to Ben. "Now we wait for the fun to start . . ." He reached over and made sure that the window was open as wide as it would go. A moment later there was a scuffling noise, and Toby and Bart peeped over the sill.

Max held his hand under Bart's mouth.

BURRRP! A big hairy spider with red spots fell onto his palm. It was the best one yet.

"Now, do something to get Arabella's attention," Max told Ben as the spider ran up and down his arm. "And be quick. It won't last long."

"OK," said Ben, grabbing the banana from Max's tray. "Watch this, Arabella!" he called. He expertly balanced the banana on his nose and pranced up and down in front of her.

Ben's sister turned to tell him off and Max seized his chance. He reached over and carefully put the spider under a lettuce leaf on Arabella's plate.

Ben sat down again. The boys hunched over their lunches, trying not to laugh.

"**YAAAARRRGHHH!**"

Arabella leaped into the air and her plate went flying. Her friend was showered with lettuce and tomatoes.

"What's all this noise?"

"Mrs Hogsbum!" warned Max as the

head teacher loomed over them.

"There was a huge spider on my plate," whimpered Arabella. "Ben and Max put it there. They've got a trick one."

Ben put on his most innocent face. "I can't see a spider," he said. "And you took away my toy one, Arabella, even though I begged you not to." He turned sorrowful eyes on the head teacher. "It's in her pocket."

Mrs Hogsbottom glared at him suspiciously. She looked like a vulture with toothache. Out of the corner of his eye, Max saw the spider peep out from under the lettuce leaf and then disappear into thin air.

Just in time! Mrs Hogsbum examined the mess on the table with her laser vision. "I've looked through this salad," she announced, "and there is no evidence of a spider."

She frowned at Ben's sister. "You have broken school rule number forty-eight: pupils must not pretend there are spiders at the dinner table." She shook her head. "I thought you would know how to behave, Arabella Neal. If you're not careful, I will have to take back your monitor's badge." She turned on her heel and left.

Arabella threw the boys a furious look and then flounced off with her friend.

Max heard a chortling. Toby and Bart were rolling about on the window ledge.

"That's my best trick since I put spiders down the vicar's socks," said Bart.

Ben pushed the chocolate pudding over to Max and the gargoylz. "You deserve this," he said with a grin. "I don't think we'll have any more trouble from my big sister."

"Who'd have thought late lunch could turn out so well?" laughed Max, his mouth full of yummy chocolateyness.

"Dangling drainpipes!" chuckled Toby as he and Bart took mouthfuls of chocolate pudding. "You two are as mischievous as gargoylz!"

4. Now You See It, Now You Don't!

"It's Friday!" said Max as he and Ben zoomed in through the school gates on their imaginary spy spaceship. "You know what that means . . ."

"No school for two days!" yelled Ben, punching the air.

"But we won't see Toby for two days either," Max reminded him.

Ben skidded to a halt. "I didn't think of that," he said with a frown.

Max looked up at the school roof and then over to the church for their gargoyle friend. "Can't see him," he said. "That's funny. He's usually around when we get here."

"No time to find him now," said Ben as a scrawny, witch-like figure marched towards them. "Here comes Horrible Hogsbum to chase us in."

Toby didn't appear at playtime either. Max and Ben looked everywhere. They even rummaged through the PE store cupboard, where they got caught by Miss Bleet; they had to sweep it out as a punishment.

After lunch they burst into the playground.
"He's got to be somewhere," said Ben.

"Maybe he's gone on holiday or
something," suggested Max.

The boys peered over the wall into the
churchyard. The place was full of old grey
tombstones covered in ivy.

Ben suddenly let out a cry. "There he is!"

The little monkey-faced gargoyle
was sitting hunched in
the long grass
behind one of the
tombstones. His
wings were folded
close to his body and
he had a wicked grin
on his face.

"Hey, Toby!" yelled
Max, waving. "Over
here!"

Toby whipped round. "*Shhhh*," he hissed.
"I'm hiding from Zackary."

Max looked up and down the churchyard. "I can't see any other gargoylz," he whispered to Ben. "I think he's tricking us."

At that moment Toby was suddenly flung up into the air. He gave a yelp of surprise, somersaulted three times and landed on his bottom. Then he picked himself up and scampered over to perch on a huge stone slab near Max and Ben.

"Greetingz!" he said in his growly purr. "Zackary and I were playing hide-and-seek.

You haven't met my friend Zackary before. Say hello to my humanz, Zack." He waved a paw at the empty space beside him.

"Have you gone mad, Toby?" asked Max, scratching his head. "There's no one there."

POP! Max and Ben jumped in surprise as a grinning gargoyle appeared out of thin air. He had a fuzzy mane and a tuft on his head and he dashed up and down like an eager puppy, his eyes flashing everywhere as if he was looking for mischief.

"Morning," he said, bounding over to the boys. "Wait a sec – you're humanz. Got to be scared of humanz! Wait a sec – you're friendly humanz. Toby told me. Nice to meet you." His words came out in a rush.

"You can make yourself invisible," gasped Ben.

"Of course!" panted Zack. "Special power." He faded in and out of view a few times. "It's easy. Can't humanz do it?"

"I wish we could," sighed Max.

"Isn't it a bit difficult to play hide-and-seek with Zack?" Ben asked Toby. "How do you ever find him?"

Toby laughed. "He's not invisible to gargoylz – only humanz."

"But how did he creep up on you like that if you can see him?" said Max.

"He's very sneaky," said Toby, "and he raced up behind me."

"I won, I won!" chanted Zack, bouncing up and down on his big floppy paws and panting loudly. "I hid the longest."

"We agreed that whoever won the game would get out of food collecting at the weekend," explained Toby.

"You did two minutes," crowed Zack, slapping Toby on the back and knocking him off the slab. "I did *twenty*."

"But that wasn't fair," protested Toby as he flew back up. "You wouldn't have known where I was if these two hadn't given the game away."

"S'pose so," grumbled Zack. "Wait a sec – call it a draw then!"

"OK, we'll both get the food tomorrow," agreed Toby. They shook paws.

"Can we help?" asked Max eagerly. "We don't have school on Saturday.

SECRET CODEWORD: TRICK

What do gargoylz eat anyway?"

"Bramblz!" said Toby.

"Thistlz!" cried Zack. "Anything with pricklz!" declared Toby in a sing-song voice. Then he added, "Rose thornz are particularly yummy, and Zack here loves stinging nettlz, don't you, Zack?"

But Zack had gone. He was bouncing over the tombstones, chanting, "Bramblz, thistlz, anything with pricklz!" as he went. He kept disappearing and then reappearing in unexpected places.

"I've got a brilliant idea!" said Max suddenly. "There are loads of brambles at the bottom of my nan's garden." Toby sat up eagerly. "We could take you and Zack there tomorrow. As long as she doesn't see you, you can get all the food you like."

"Spluttering gutterz!" exclaimed Toby. "That would be marvellous."

"You can try my nan's cupcakes as well," Max told him. "They're *her* special power!"

"Everyone loves them," agreed Ben.

Zack zoomed by at high speed. Toby
stuck out a leg, tripped him up and sat on
him. He told him Max's idea.

"And there might even be some
stingers," Max added.

"Yummmm," murmured Zack, his eyes
glazing over in delight. "Bramblz, thistlz,
anything with pricklz."

The bell rang for afternoon school.

"Oh, no!" groaned Ben. "We've got

history with Mr Oldhart now. Why do we have to have him every Friday afternoon? He's so ancient he was around with the dinosaurs. He's bound to tell us about something really boring like Stone Age soup recipes or Queen Mary's petticoats!"

"But that's not the worst thing," moaned Max. "Old Fart always gives us *loads* of homework. We won't have time to go bramble hunting at Nan's after all."

"Unless," said Ben thoughtfully, "we get Zack to make himself invisible and then rub out all the homework that Old Fart writes up on the board. We can't do any then, can we?"

"And we'd be doing him a favour really," added Max excitedly, "because he won't have all that marking on Monday!"

"You're nearly as good as gargoylz at thinking up tricks," said Toby with a sigh of admiration.

"I love tricks!" yelled Zack. "Can't wait."

"I'll get my bag," said Max, "so we can smuggle Zack into class." He raced away and was soon back with his rucksack.

Zack zoomed twice round the churchyard and leaped head first into the open bag. "Let's go!" came his muffled voice.

Max and Ben grinned at each other. This was going to be a great trick!

The two boys made their way into class and sat at a table right underneath Mr Oldhart's nose. Max made sure he put his bag down out of sight.

"I don't like it at the front," Ben whispered with a shudder. "Gives me the heebie-jeebies."

Mr Oldhart put a pile of grey books down on his desk. He arranged his pens in

a circle around his glasses case and blew
his nose loudly. Then he began to drone
on. Max and Ben watched the hands of
the clock tick slowly round.

"This is the most boring history lesson
in the history of boring history lessons,"
muttered Max, his head in his hands.
"Who cares about basket weaving in the
Middle Ages?"

"And we're too near Old Fart to have

a pencil fight," groaned Ben. "Or even a rubber-flicking contest."

"Now, class, the moment you've all been waiting for," announced Mr Oldhart at last, his eyes gleaming. "I'm going to

write your homework instructions on the board for you to copy down. While I'm doing it, I want you to draw a picture of the wicker basket on page eleven. I know you're all eager, but take your time. One should never rush a picture of a wicker basket."

Max sprang into action. He knocked
his pencil to the floor and stuck his head
under the table, pretending to look for it.
"Get ready, Zack!" he whispered into his
rucksack.

There was a shuffling noise and a fuzzy
mane appeared.

"You're supposed to be invisible!" Max
reminded the excited gargoyle. There was
a faint **pop** and Zack vanished.

Mr Oldhart filled the board with
homework and turned back to the class.
"I've given you plenty to keep you busy
till Monday," he said happily. "I wouldn't

want you getting bored over the weekend."

The class read the instructions, realized there would be hours of work, and groaned.

"I knew you'd be pleased." Mr Oldhart beamed.

"Go, Zack!" whispered Max.

Very soon every trace of homework had disappeared, wiped away by an invisible paw. Max and Ben could hardly keep straight faces; their classmates couldn't keep straight faces at all. They were soon laughing and pointing at the blank whiteboard.

"Oh, no!" groaned Ben. "He'll see what's happened before it's time to go home."

Mr Oldhart turned to the board. He took off his glasses and rubbed his eyes. "I could have sworn I put the homework up there just now," he muttered.

He sighed and wrote it up for a second time, but as soon as he turned back to his

table, the words disappeared again. This time everyone except Max and Ben was busily copying the picture of the basket, so they didn't notice. Max held his breath. Perhaps Old Fart wouldn't notice that the homework had vanished either. But, to his dismay, their teacher suddenly swung round to the board.

"I quite forgot to put up question twenty-three . . ." he murmured. Then he stopped and stared at the board in disbelief. "Who did that?" he demanded.

"Did what, sir?" asked Ben innocently.

"Someone has rubbed the homework off the board," Mr Oldhart said, peering suspiciously at Ben and Max. "Mrs Hogsbottom warned me about you two.

Have you boys got something to do with this?"

"Not us, sir," said Max. "We haven't left our chairs."

Mr Oldhart sighed deeply and turned back to the board. He wrote all the homework up for a third time and then sat and watched the class closely.

"This isn't working," whispered Ben. "How can we stop him from noticing the empty board when Zack rubs out the writing?"

"Hmm . . ." Max murmured. Then, "Got it!" he whispered. He bent down and pretended to get something out of his bag. "Zack!" he said softly. "This time, can you write different words up there instead, so that Old Fart won't see an empty board? You can write, can't you?"

Zack stuck his head out eagerly. "Course I can, silly human!"

"Then give us some really fun homework," said Max.

"With plenty of football," added Ben.

POP! Zack disappeared.

And a few seconds later, so did the writing on the board.

Max looked around. Everyone had their heads bent over their books. Mr Oldhart was still glaring at the class. Max glanced back at the board. To his delight, new words were being scribbled all over it, but then he realized that he could see something else too . . .

"Oh, no!" he muttered to Ben. "Zack's tail has appeared!"

Ben looked up. Now the boys could see little claws and the hint of a mane.

"As soon as you've finished your
picture, you can copy down the homework
instructions," Mr Oldhart told the class.
A worried look crossed his face and he
turned to glance at the board. Max caught
his breath nervously, but, in the nick of
time, Zack skittered away from the board

and threw himself into the rucksack. Mr Oldhart looked back at the class, clearly satisfied that the homework was still there for all to see.

"He didn't notice that the words are different," whispered Max.

"Better do as he says then," grinned Ben.

Along with the rest of the class, the boys grabbed their pencils and carefully wrote down – 'Play lots of football, hide-and-seek and pranks. Have lots of fun!'

The bell rang. School was over for another week. Everyone in the class grabbed their bags and ran out of the room, giggling at Mr Oldhart's surprising choice of homework. Max made sure Zack

was safely inside his rucksack and then
made a bolt for the door, Ben at his heels.

"Football? Hide-and-seek? *Pranks?*"
they heard Mr Oldhart splutter as they
dashed out of the classroom. He had
finally read the board.

The boys had just escaped round the corner when a dreadful figure loomed up in front of them. It was Mrs Hogsbottom.

"Uh-oh!" muttered Max. "Do you think she can have found out about the homework?"

Mrs Hogsbottom planted herself in front of the boys, one hand behind her back. "Aren't you forgetting something, Ben?" she boomed.

"Er . . . no . . . It wasn't us who . . ." stammered Ben.

"Rule seven," said Mrs Hogsbottom, producing Ben's football from behind her back. "Head teachers always return footballs when they say they will."

"Thanks Mrs Hogsbu— ttom!" said Ben, grabbing it.

Outside in the playground, Max and Ben sprinted across to the wall by the churchyard. Making sure that no one was looking, Max put down his bag and let Zack out. The little gargoyle scampered over the wall, where Toby was waiting to hear all about it.

Zack told him what had happened – acting out the best bits all around the churchyard.

When he'd finished, Toby patted him on the head. "That's the best trick you've played since you juggled the hymn books and frightened the vicar," he said proudly. Then he waggled a finger at Max and Ben.

"You two had better go home and get on with that homework!"

"We'll start right now," said Ben seriously, and he spun his football on one finger.

"And tomorrow we'll take you to Nan's and give you your treat," added Max.

"Bramblz, thistlz, anything with pricklz!" yelled Zack. "You should try them too!"

The boys laughed.

"I think we'll stick to Nan's cupcakes, thanks," Max said with a grin.

Gargoylz Fact File

Full name: Tobias the Third

Known as: Toby

Special Power: Flying

Likes: All kinds of pranks and mischief – especially playing jokes on the vicar

Dislikes: Mrs Hogsbottom

Full name: Barnabas

Known as: Barney

Special Power: Making big stinks!

Likes: Cookies

Dislikes: Being surprised by humanz

Full name: Bartholomew

Known as: Bart

Special Power:
Burping spiders

Likes: Being grumpy

Dislikes: Being told to cheer up

Full name: Zackary

Known as: Zack

Special Power: Making himself invisible to humanz

Likes: Bouncing around, eating bramblz, thistlz, and anything with pricklz!

Dislikes: Keeping still